STUPID IN MONTANA
AS AMERICA

ROBERT E. MILLIKEN

Outskirts Press, Inc.
Denver, Colorado

Author's Note

Between you and me, I've been stupid, too.

Like the time I rode a motorcycle from Idaho Falls to Baker for twenty-two hours straight.

I was twenty-six years old, and after leaving Las Vegas before the sunrise, I rode another one and a half hours. I was coming into Baker at seventy miles per hour with the morning sun on my back and sound asleep.

And to this day I believe an angel awoke me just before I laid myself over a guardrail and ripped myself apart.

Never in my life had I been so scared, so I cranked it up to ninety and got to Baker, holding one eye open with my left hand and steering with my right, looking for a place to sleep as I didn't have time to check into a room.

Finally I found a spot of grass behind Bun Boy restaurant next to the Dumpster and slept for a few hours while I could have easily been robbed. I mean they could have taken everything, including the clothes I was wearing, and I wouldn't have woken up. Now that was stupid, but we learn from our mistakes. It's just that some of us have to have more than others.

Introduction

I've been inspired to write this book in the hopes that perhaps this is good timing, and even though it's a problem that most of us are already aware of, perhaps by reading this we will band together and do something more than the usual—turn our heads and look the other way—or at the very least feel inspired to start changing ourselves. Personally I have sought to improve myself spiritually, intellectually, and physically my whole life, since I believe that is what I'm here for, in this incarnation, and not what I see so many others doing, which brings me to this book.

Contents

CHAPTER 1
Let's Get Ya Hot

I'm here to tell you that when I'm in a foreign country and I see an average American, I may have a deferent different view point than of the local's who live there.

I think it's probably a form of the ugly, irresponsible, possibly self-inflicted human nature thing called prejudice that I have been conditioned to. And why? Because I've lived here in the United States for all my life and I've seen how they act, how they walk, how they drive their cars, shop, eat, drink, swim, ride. You name it.

Stupid In Montana As America

And after all my attempts at trying to justify their actions or the things they say, like, Oh, he just said that because no one has ever told him different, but he's not a bad guy, or she just has a lot on her mind, that's why she left the shopping cart in the center of the aisle, but she's smiling so she's not so bad, and she and him probably aren't bad people; in fact they might be really good people—they're just stupid.

But the foreigner doesn't see them that way; he sees them as belonging to the most sophisticated and rich country with the most powerful military on the planet, and in a sense they are, except they didn't really design all that stuff or create that awesome economy that enabled their parents to put them through college, which got them that job and bought them that airline ticket. They're just taxpayers and lucky, lucky to be born there.

You know, it used to be that if you had money and it wasn't inherited, it meant that you were probably a highly intelligent and sophisticated type with good business sense.

But nowadays you can be one of the stupidest people

on the entire planet and drive a brand-new SUV and have an airline ticket.

And if you're really pissed off or, rather, stimulated into reading more, then for sure you're going to be stupid. Or on the other hand you may be pleasantly pleased to know that there's someone else out there who feels the same way you do.

But if you're not stupid, then don't be mad at me because I didn't do it and I can't fix it, but I can fix myself, and even though I'm no genius, I do know that when I come to a situation like where to park my shopping cart because someone else might be coming along since it's a public place and, hey, they might even be walking down this aisle since all the stuff on the shelves couldn't be just for me, I think, *Duh.*

So now here you are thinking, I don't do that when I come to a situation—I think it through, and maybe you do or maybe you just think you do or maybe you just don't care, but if that's the case then stop reading since you probably won't understand this book anyway. But you may instead just do what is called a conditioned response, which would make you a typical, average American or, better yet, a typical, average American dog.

But don't let that make you hot, because if you're a typical, average American, then you're probably highly trained in the art of conditioned response.

And as for thinking, well, that's something we'll leave up to the scientists. They can make some sort of pill or something to take care of that.

That's right up there with *I think I'll have lots of kids and buy a big house and go on living life as good since the world is an endless supply of resources and even though we're at possibly seven billion people in the world, life will go on forever and ever, and why? Well, because.*

Thinking. That's the one thing that nobody said anything about in school. I mean, they used the word and told us to think, but they didn't teach purity of thought and thought cleansing or, least of all, thought stimulation.

Now, you might be one of those saying to yourself, *Rob's an idiot. I think all the time, like, I think I'm going to the store, but when I get there I'll park in one and a half parking spots even though the parking lot is full, and I don't think it will matter,* "don't think" being the key words. Or *I don't think it's my fault when someone pulls out in front of me when they can clearly see me coming, even though I am speeding.* Again, don't think.

By now you're probably thinking, *He's wrong, most people in this country are fairly intelligent,* but I say, Oh yeah? Then why is it that when I'm driving on a winding mountain road that runs alongside a lake with a double yellow line for ten miles, and the speed limit is sixty miles per hour, and my average speed is sixty-three miles per hour, ninety-nine percent of all the drivers going in the same direction will climb on my ass. Then when I slow down, which I always do, they will just sit there on my ass, unable to figure out why I have slowed down and unable to figure out whether to back off so I can speed back up, or pass.

In fact, they typically get even closer, totally incapable of figuring it out, and I'm pretty sure they are back there saying, Look at this idiot. He's going forty-five in a sixty; and I am up in front saying, Too stupid to pass, just

5

too stupid.

It's times like this I wish all vehicles were equipped with short distance radios so I could say something colorful and short and to the point, like, Hey, stupid, the reason I've slowed down is because you're on my ass, you incredible idiot.

And then after miles and miles of this we come to a place in the road where it's legal to pass and totally safe since you can see that there is no oncoming traffic for a half mile down the road at forty-five miles per hour, and the idiot just sits there staring at my bumper (in, I might add, one of the most beautiful places I know) completely void of thought like a mindless barbarian, without the barbarism. Unless a deer jumps out in front of me and I have to slam on my brakes so that he rear-ends me and we both go off the road, rolling and taking out the guardrail and trees with twisted metal igniting on fire.

And you think, *Hey, that does look like barbarism.*

Very rarely do I have a person come on my ass who has enough mind capacity to figure out why I slowed down and then back off; in fact it's extremely rare.

Let's Get Ya Hot

So what is it, lack of caring or maybe just plain laziness? I think neither. After years of careful analysis I've come to the conclusion that it's just plain stupid, and if stupid is a form of a disease, then this nation is deeply infected to a critical level, and why shouldn't it be a disease? They say alcoholism is, and then like alcoholism, stupidity is a progressive and incurable disease also.

Except that's the old way of thinking. The new way, thanks to Allen Carr, the author of *The Easy Way to Stop Drinking,* is that alcoholism is curable; in fact, it's one of the easiest to cure and so should be stupidity, but like alcoholism most people with stupid need to hit bottom first.

And that is what it appears to be in many cases.

Have you ever thought to find out how long it takes after you start on your way in your automobile on any average day before you come across an idiot doing something really stupid?

Well, I have, and if I'm in the city, which I usually am in the wintertime, I have found that it typically takes about three to five minutes. Every single time. It's extremely rare for me to go anywhere without seeing some-one do something stupid, and I'm not talking about old people who are so old that their minds are gone, or young people whose hormones are running so rampant that they can't see straight.

I'm talking about people in their late twenties to late sixties when all their faculties should still be there.

It's amazing. I walk around in awe at these people all the time; literally everywhere I go I see it—American stupidity.

I'm almost fifty years old. I've lived in Montana now for twenty years, and I've been in and out of Montana for about thirty-two years, and I've got to tell you, I've seen a lot of change. We have a tremendous influx of people coming in to live the Montana dream of beautiful views, unrestrained roads, and peace and quiet, including the fishing, hunting, day hiking, cleaner air, etc.

Yep, there are people here from all over the United States, and on any given day in the summertime you can drive around here and see multiple different license plates.

Which is great, except the vast majority of them are conditioned to the lifestyles they've been living, and they can't change since they don't seem to have the ability to stop and think, *Hey, maybe since I'm in Rome I should observe how the Romans act, drive, walk, run, or jump, and then do like the Romans do.*

They can't, on arriving here, stop and think, *Hey, maybe instead of running to my car in the morning and getting to work as soon as I can, I should stop and take a deep breath of air, smell the wonderful aromas, and take my time driving to work so I can look out my window and see all the beautiful sights.*

I'm amazed, and to give you an idea of what I'm talking about, a few years back I was driving down the road on my way to work in my usual not-in-any-hurry-to-get-there mode of operation, when I saw a bear out my driver's side window, which for me is great since I love to see bears, and as my brother once said, any day you see a bear is a good day.

So I looked up into my rearview mirror and I see the idiot who had been speeding approach my ass, which I

9

assume is an attempt to push or force me to speed up past the speed limit, and I see him looking at my bumper, totally unaware of the bear on his left.

So naturally I think to myself, *Idiot,* and hit my brakes, slow down, and proceed to look for more wildlife while the idiot behind me stares at my bumper.

I just shake my head, as this is not an unusual experience here in Montana anymore, but why is he here? There isn't a lot of money to be made here, so why would you be in a hurry to get to work, or better yet, why would you even be here working if you're not interested in Montana, the outdoors, I mean? It just doesn't make any sense.

Personally if I didn't care about the views out my windows on the way to work or wherever I was going, I most certainly wouldn't be in Montana. Hell, I would be in a city like LA where the money is.

But then that's me. I make sense of things.

And the sense to be made about the guy who's staring at a bumper when there's a bear to be seen is simple: he's stupid.

Let's Get Ya Hot

Yep, any given day you can take a walk on just about any given trail here in Montana, and it's just a matter of time before you come upon a person coming the opposite direction with a vicious dog who has a look in his eye like he would love to bite you, and he snarls and barks and speeds toward you in a highly aggressive manner. So you begin to back up and at the same time the owners yell, Don't worry, he doesn't bite, and you think, *What an idiot.* What they're really doing is telling the dog that it's okay, as the dog has been conditioned to know it's okay when his owners say, Don't worry, he doesn't bite. And it's too late, you're already upset, but they're too stupid to know that, so you move off, thinking, *Where are these people coming from,* knowing it's from somewhere in America.

They possibly even graduated from high school or even college, and now here they are walking down a trail being outsmarted by their dog.

Every year more and more people come here to get away from where they've been living, and every year they just get dumber and dumber. It's as if they don't know any better because their parents didn't know any better, and their parents before them did, but somehow didn't get the message across.

A few years ago I was on my favorite lake, fishing for northerns, which is a term that refers to northern pike, and I had gotten into my small one-man pontoon boat and oared out to one of my favorite weed beds. The water was calm, the sky held scattered clouds, and the day was mild. There were a few other fishermen on the shoreline and some kids playing on the shore, with their parents drinking their favorite beverages.

I felt very fortunate to be there. The pike were slamming my artificial lure one after the other, averaging four to ten pounds, and I was having a great time. Then along came these two guys on wave runners at a top speed of around seventy miles per hour.

They kept coming all the way in, to around two hundred feet from shore on both sides of me, with the one on the right side of me at about ninety feet away. He proceeded to maneuver his machine into a tight circle, so tight that for about five minutes he went around and around with his body horizontal and his head below the natural level of water. Now, I looked at this person and I could see that he was in his late twenties to early thirties, and as he continued this maneuver he created a siphoning effect on the bottom, tearing up the weeds and bringing the mud to the surface.

Well, needless to say, my first thought was to cast my lure at him in an attempt to hook him and pull him off the machine, but instead, I took a deep breath and calmed down, deciding to take the high road, only to look around and see that everyone else was pissed off as well and probably hoping that I was going to do something, since I was closest.

Then he stopped, straightened it out, and shot between me and the shore, hooked up with his buddy, and they both shot across the lake out of sight.

Needless to say the fishing was shut off, as the lake calmed back down and the floating weeds and mud dispersed in all directions.

As for me, the day was over, and I wondered where these guys could be from. Where in the world would I go to find someone who is so stupid as to not understand the concept of fishing and the common courtesy that goes with it? Our God-given, inalienable right, our heritage. The Brazilian rain forest? It has been said that the Amazon Indians are some of the most backward and stupid people on the planet.

But wait, I don't think that you could find a Brazilian Indian who was so backward and so stupid as to not understand the concept of peace and quiet while fishing, let alone to not understand that it is just good manners to keep a certain distance from a person while they are fishing, so where I ask?

The next day I am milling about in town and I hear the Syrian going off, and the Quick Response Unit is dispatched to an accident on the road by the lake.

It turns out that these two young men had driven up to the local gas station at the north end of the lake and purchased fifteen gallons of probably high octane gas, placed it in the back of their SUV, and proceeded to drive on the winding mountain lake road back to their cabin on the lake, drinking beer and smoking cigarettes. When, imagine this, something happened, and they swerved off the road, crashing into the hillside.

And as they came to an abrupt stop, all that gas in the rear of the vehicle came flying forward, dowsing them and the whole front of the vehicle compartment and igniting from the burning cigarettes.

Miraculously they both managed to exit the vehicle and run across the road, over the guardrail, down the rocky shore completely on fire, and plunge into the water, where the one probably passed out and drowned due to massive shock, as they found his body in sixty feet of water, and the other somehow survived with over ninety percent of his body burned.

So I ask, where did these guys come from?

They weren't teenagers with hormones going berserk or ninety-year-olds who couldn't see, smell, taste, or feel anything, so where and how?

All I can say is incredible, or better yet, and seemingly my favorite words, how incredibly stupid.

It's almost incomprehensible how some people can be thirty years old and live in this country and not know how dangerous gasoline and cigarettes and drinking and driving, not to mention winding mountain roads, are.

Now that's three hundred and sixty-five days in a year, times thirty, times hours in a day, which comes to two hundred and sixty-two thousand hours they had to learn that gasoline is dangerous.

Or perhaps they knew it was dangerous but forgot to think.

Or perhaps they had been talking their whole lives and had never listened to anyone ever, or perhaps God just didn't give them even remotely as many brain cells as the rest of us.

Well, at any rate it was two idiots in the same place at the same time.

Actually I might have a theory. I've been thinking that it might have something to do with the fact that there's less oxygen per air mass in the world today, and our brains are suffering from an insufficient supply of oxygen to our brain cells.

Of course anyone can be negative, and I apologize for sounding so gloomy, but as I'm sure you know it's hard.

Let's Get Ya Hot

And I would like you to know that I am not the kind of person who normally verbalizes anything negative about the dead. I believe that if you don't have anything nice to say about them, you shouldn't say anything at all, as I don't need to beat them up—they're dead.

The Indians believe it's impolite and I agree, but if I can say something that only helps one soul in the whole universe then it is worth it and I will.

And I have said some bad things in my time, like, what if the terrorists made a bomb that only killed stupid people, and that would be really bad, because for one thing…even though they would be the first to go…there wouldn't be hardly anyone left to carry on the human enterprise.

Anyway, there probably has always been ignorance and stupidity in the world, but never on today's scale, per capita I mean.

Just the other day, I was standing in a line inside a gas station waiting for the longest time to pay for my gas, when the cashier finally came back in from the outside, and she said, "Sorry for the wait, but there was someone out there whom I needed to show how to push a button."

I quickly smiled and responded,

"Well, it was probably an American."

Her jaw dropped as if she couldn't believe I said that, but also because I hit the nail on the head, and she's used to it. The average person who goes in there and does something stupid is either an American or a Canadian, simply because we live near the Canadian border and there are lots of them around here.

But what I was proud of was the speed at which I conveyed that message, as it's speed that often makes for good humor.

It's interesting that the further we go into the future and the more people we have, the dumber we are, thus the more people we get since it's dumb to have children when we can't even take care of the ones we have already.

And at the same time we have more access to motorized vehicles, so what we have is a whole bunch of people moving around in heavy and high-speed motorized vehicles without a brain. We need to start making vehicles that have a brain and can think for us, so that way we are not allowed to do stupid things when we are moving about, since our vehicles won't let us.

But most importantly we won't need a brain, which saves a lot of effort.

We can have smart vehicles so we don't have to think on the road and smart houses so we don't have to think when we get home or when we leave in the morning and even smart jobs so we don't even have to think at work.

Then that way all we have to do is pay taxes and make babies so they can grow up and keep paying the taxes, and all the smart people can keep making smart machines, and around and around we go until there are fewer and fewer smart people.

That is seemingly one of the directions we are headed, but at any rate the one good thing is that it might weed out the Stupid Money.

Or at least we won't notice it so much, which would be good for me because that Stupid Money really makes me sick.

And that's what's coming to Montana in droves and

multitudes. We want the money, but we don't want the stupid that comes with it. It's a real rock in a hard place.

To give you an idea of what I mean about Stupid Money, a friend of mine was telling me that he had been golfing last spring on one of the local courses with some associates of his—and keep in mind this is one of the more expensive of the many courses in the area—while he exclaimed that they could hear spring tom turkeys gobbling in the background, since at this particular course there are a lot of turkeys, geese, deer, and an assortment of wildlife.

Suddenly one of the group said, "What is that sound?"

And my friend said, "Do you mean that sound?"

And she said, "Yeah," as a spring gobbler gobbled, and he exclaimed, "Oh, that's a turkey."

And she said, "Oh."

Well, by now you know how my mind works, but I have just got to tell you anyway that I immediately began to ponder where this person could have come from, but figuring she was from this country, I asked, "How old is this person," and he answered, "Oh, probably around fifty-five."

I said, "Wow."

So from there I have pondered how someone could live in this country and be so stupid as to not know what a turkey sounds like, with Thanksgiving and the Thanksgiving decorations, the advertisements on television, and the talking turkeys on the table and in the stores.

How is it possible that a bipedal humanoid with a brain living in the United States could not know what a turkey sounds like?

Then I realized they can't, I mean with the brain part. So I tried to relate her to my family and all the Thanksgivings we had together. I began to associate her with various members, and then I started to imagine the one who everybody liked and was always happy and gleeful, perhaps was kind and gentle and easy to talk to, but never really said anything.

Keeping in mind that I come from a pretty big family, to do this imagining is quite an undertaking, but upon completion I can't imagine anyone in my family who could be that stupid, or for that matter I can't imagine anyone from this country, and of course I mean of that time, twenty years ago, since that's how long it's been since I've had Thanksgiving with my family as they live far, far away from here.

So once again I'll just turn my head and walk the other way since it's probably just too late to fix this person anyway, and I imagine her family gave up on her a long time ago.

They say alcoholism is a disease, and if that's so then I think that stupidity is one too, and looking at it in that sense changes our perspective on it completely. I have noticed that it has similar traits and symptoms of a disease in that a person can start out perfectly healthy and do well in school, graduate, get married, have kids, and the kids grow up and leave home, and the parents are stupid; in fact, the whole family is.

But not always. In many cases just the parents are, and so for years I've wondered if raising kids makes you stupid, but that doesn't make any sense. I mean, how could one person make another stupid? Well, he couldn't, so that's what brought me to the thinking that it's a disease and these people became infected shortly after school.

I've noticed some people can become infected as single people do, but it's rare—usually it's married types. It's like they came down with a bad cold and kept giving it back to each other; right when one would be getting over it, they would get too close or something to the other and become infected again, and over and over and over again, and then one day they wake up and go out into the world and say or do something that's so stupid it makes you ponder for weeks why they said that or what they were thinking.

But the conclusion is always the same and it's because they weren't thinking, because they were stupid. Or perhaps it would be better put that they *have* stupid. Just like when a person has cancer, you say they *have* cancer, not they *are* cancer.

At this point I'm going to blame the school system, but not as a whole since I believe nothing is perfect, but nothing is all bad, either, and I am sure there are many professors out there who do teach and stimulate the part of the brain that wonders.

Which brings me to the problem, I think, that the school system in a large part teaches a lot of information and how to calculate, simulate, and process that information, but they don't stimulate the part of the brain that wonders.

They don't seem to give students a desire to ponder the secrets of the universe, and I don't mean for a short period of time like Oh, I wondered this or I wondered that and now I'm done.

No, I mean each student should leave school pondering their own particular interest until it has been acquired, and if not achievable then move on to another and another. Then having the desire to know more, and that being so strong that they can't stop, they move on to another subject, and on and on and so on for the rest of their lives.

And I know that many people do this, as they are called smart people, which is why I need to emphasize the word *each* as in each and every student, and that they should not be able to graduate until they have demonstrated that they will continue to ponder things for the rest of their lives.

That way, when they do something simple like driving down the road, they have the ability to think and/or equate when something that's not in the driving manual occurs. Thus, instead of them sitting back there behind me at only one or two car lengths going *Duh, why is he going so slow*, instead, they could think, *Hey, maybe I should pass this guy since he's probably going slower because I'm following too closely.*

Thought process is the one thing that separates us from the animal kingdom.

An act of war

This is thought to be a tribe of Brazilian Indians who have never had contact with the outside world. This picture was taken from an airplane and shows their reaction to an over flight of their camp. According to the article this picture came from, the Indians actually loosed arrows in the year 2007.

CHAPTER 2
A Piece Of Me

These Americans today, I tell ya; when I was a young man, I was normal, in that I had all the hormonal changes and imbalances going on. Yep, until I was twenty it seems as though all I thought about was girls.

It was like one big chase race, and the one who met the most girls in the end won.

But then I started to grow up, I took real estate courses and money seminars, I worked as a carpenter, and that paid the bills and put food on the table. I started reading and I acquired goals and continued to better myself both spiritually and physically and continue to this day, unlike so many others.

Stupid In Montana As America

Very few people I have known continue to improve themselves their whole lives. It's like they get to a point and that is it, they're done, they are all they can be, and they're happy with that, and for some that point seems to have occurred at a very young age.

It's especially prevalent in ex college students, especially the ten-year ones; it's as though they have worked too hard to stay that long, and so when they graduate, it's like we are smart now and that's it, they're done.

And typically they are some of the stupidest people I have ever known.

They're like the big rock that rolls off the hill into the river below and sits there all tough, making the water go around, but time tells all, and sure enough in time, it withers away. Just like their brains, they get out of college and that's it, they slowly wither.

Very seldom do you meet someone who is on that path to be the most they can their whole life; in fact, I think that most fall off of it at a young age, and that may be the root of the problem.

People get so caught up in their lives that they forget

life should be a quest of improvement until the end, and I don't mean up until twenty-seven—get married and have kids and forget about it until the kids leave home. I mean every second of every hour of your life, always.

Which brings me to my average day. I wake up in the morning and do my usual, you know, bathroom stuff, coffee, scratch my head, and rub my eyes, and off I go.

Get in my car, go down the road about three to five minutes, and *bam*, I say to myself, What an idiot, there's a guy going down the road speeding and running the stop, and he proceeds to break any and every driving rule and then goes on speeding again, and why? Could it be that he has an important assignment, like maybe he's a member of the Secret Service, and he's late to meet up with the other Secret Service members to protect the president as he arrives in just fifteen minutes, and it takes twenty minutes to get there?

Or maybe it's even more important, like he's got the president in the car with him and he's doing a strategic maneuver to get away from a would-be assassin.

And then *bam*, he pulls into the local grocery store

parking lot because he needs some milk with his cereal this morning, and "The Jeffersons" are on and he's only seen this episode fifty or sixty times.

But that's worth it to risk his and everyone else's life. I think not. What I really think is that he got up that morning and didn't think at all about the consequences of breaking all the driving rules and regulations, because even though he studied for, and passed, the driver's examination, the materials never said anything at all about processing thought at the same time as you're driving a motorized vehicle, so it's not his fault, it's his parents' fault, or better yet it's society's fault. I mean, he's just in a hurry with nowhere important to be, not knowing why, just going through life like everyone else, you know, paying bills, raising kids. What else is there?

So then I get down the road a little further, and I look in the rearview mirror, and here is someone on my ass, so I look at the speedometer and see that I'm going the speed limit, so I do as I always do—I slow down. Naturally since the speed laws were made for normal conditions, and having someone on your ass is not safe or a normal condition, I must slow down.

And then we come to a place in the road where they can pass and pass safely, but they don't, and why? I can only come up with one explanation, and that's that they're stupid, and why are they stupid? Because they don't have the ability to process thought.

They just sit back there on my ass and stare at my bumper, completely unable to figure out why I'm going slower than I was before they got on my ass.

So instead of carrying out a thought process and backing off so I can take it back up to the speed limit again, they get closer and I go slower and they get madder: Conditioned Response.

Not thinking for oneself. It goes all the way back to kindergarten where the teacher drew a picture of a tree and told the class to draw a tree, so we did, and the ones who drew the tree that best matched the tree on the chalkboard got the best grade rather than the ones who used imagination or pondered a more beautiful tree like the one down the road on the way to school.

Yes, that's right, they made us spend hours and hours

of our time in school learning all kinds of things like how to think but failed to teach the most important thing and that is, how to exercise thought stimulation.

They just wanted us to retain information like two plus two is four and not something a little more interesting like two red blood cells plus two red blood cells equals four universes of their own and independent of each other and why.

So now we get in the car and do something that must be as stupid as stupid gets, like risk our lives to get to a dead-end job, late because we were just too stupid to set our alarm clock five minutes ahead.

Well, I'm here to tell you, not me. I've learned through the rigors of time to use my head, thus to slow down, enjoy the view, and smell the roses.

And I don't think there's a job out there worth dying for, except of course the military or police work or the Secret Service, and in that I'm referring to risk because obviously we can't serve our country, protect our president, or enforce our laws if we're dead.

In fact, the last thing I'm going to be in a hurry for is

work. I'm in a hurry when I'm hungry to get something to eat or when I'm thirsty to get something to drink, but I'm not going to risk my life over it.

And incidentally the authorities have stated that following too close is the number one cause of traffic accidents.

Then you have these idiots who signal that they are turning and not that they are going to turn but that they are turning, and every time I see that, I think, *Idiot*, too stupid to know that he was going to turn before he started his turn, just too stupid, without common courtesy.

This, in my opinion, makes them low class as well and in a brand-new forty-eight-thousand-dollar vehicle. Imagine that. They have money but no class and they're stupid as well. Why, that would make them rich, stupid, and low class.

Then I arrive at the job, and surprisingly enough, many construction workers actually have a brain, and I know that's hard to believe since, like in the restaurant business, there are so many who don't.

Yep, in fact, in construction a person needs to be

thinking all the time or they could lose their life. Of course ninety-nine percent of the ones who do lose their life do because they weren't thinking.

And then you have my fishing. Fishing has been for almost all of my life one of my favorite pastimes. In fact, I've enjoyed it so much that it has taken me to much of the western hemisphere.

To make it short and simple, I've caught more different kinds of fish than most people have caught fish. And it goes without saying that when a person is fishing a hole on a river or a lake or wherever, you should give them a certain amount of space.

That used to be widely known, but not anymore. Now, on just about any given day, it could happen. You know, you could hike down to your favorite hole and stop, take a deep breath through your nose, and thank God for all the wonderful things in this life. Then step out into the water and tie on your favorite lure, and then look up and *bam*, you see an idiot standing at the top of your hole, casting down into it, and all the fish are shut off, as if he were dumping toxic waste into it or something. The idiot wasn't as intelligent as the fish, so he walked right up and stood on top of them.

So what I like to do is walk up to them with an awed look on my face and ask, "Where are you from," and they will typically, in an unknowing way, say something like, "Washington," and I'll say something like, "Well, did you know that I was here first and that if you stand in front of all the fish, they will see you and hide?"

And then they will say something like, "Well, this is how we do it in Washington," and I'll just shake my head and walk away and think, *Idiot, we aren't in Washington, we're in Montana.*

Yes, Montana, and here, like most other places in this country, it is apparent, the stupidity, I mean.

For me it's like looking down on earth, like at the top of a high mountain or hill at night, watching the head-lights on the cars below driving down the highways.

You will soon notice that most of them are grouped together as they go by, like three, five, two, seven, twenty, four, one, eight, and so on. What kind of animal travels in such a way?

Stupid In Montana As America

Could it be the mammalian life flora? No. Maybe fish, yeah, that's it, fish. Salmon do this on the way to their spawning grounds; their instincts are so great that when they start to migrate upriver they try to get there as quickly as possible, and it doesn't matter who's in their way.

But that's in water so that doesn't count, and then it comes to me: ants of the insect world.

If you have ever sat and watched a trail of ants you will know that they are always in a hurry, constantly rear ending, climbing over, and passing each other in an endless quest to get somewhere as quickly as possible, without knowing why.

Insects. That's why I call it insect mentality. These idiots will literally speed on a road that has a double yellow line for twenty miles to catch up to someone who is doing the speed limit, climb on their ass, and sit there until it's legal to pass. Then they pass, only to tailgate the person in front of them just a few hundred yards ahead so that there are four or six, three, fourteen, seven, one, three, all bunched up together on six hundred miles of road, just like a line of ants, hence, Insect Mentality.

But nevertheless this is still the greatest nation on the planet and I truly love this country, in spite of the simple fact that it's these same idiots that you see on the road or fishing, golfing, hiking, biking, or whatever, who are also in politics and are changing the laws of this country, which subverts and alters the very principles that made this country so great to begin with.

The gun laws are my favorite. I personally can't imagine the mind capacity it would take to think that it's possible to get guns off the street when all it takes (if you have just a fraction of my level of intellect) is to go to any hardware store and buy a few things and just make a gun in about twenty minutes, and in several different ways.

Yep, they're taking away our right to bear arms and our freedom every single day, inch by inch, and it doesn't take a mental giant to know that if a psychotic comes into a building armed with and shooting an AK-47 assault rifle, when at the same time someone in the crowd has a weapon of his own and starts returning fire, there's going to be a different outcome than if everyone's just running and hiding like sheep.

Today I was talking to a friend who just got back from Washington after being over there for three months, and it appears as though things are so bad over there now that grocery store theft is acceptable to the store, like it's part of the cost of doing business or something. I guess they just turn their heads and look the other way.

We think it's all the stupid, uneducated foreigners moving in and bringing their ways with them and our government allowing it, as if we don't have enough people in this country already.

If I had my way I would set up roadblocks, and if they want to come into this country then they would have to answer some pretty tough questions, like have them look at a picture of a banana and ask if it's a fruit or a vegetable.

Of course the problem with that is most of the people who already live here wouldn't be able to come back.

Well, maybe I'm exaggerating a little, or am I? I think I am, but then I think about the young man who walked into a mini mart looking for a job and proceeded to fill out a job application. He finished, signed it, and then robbed the store at gunpoint, and get this, then he ran home to hide at the resident address he wrote down on the application.

Yeah, that's right, he left the application there with the store clerk.

Analyzing this a little further, now, he knew how to read and write, maybe even remembered his telephone number, and he obviously remembered his address, but then he pulled a gun, forgot to think, and ran. What a Mindless Barbarian.

I'm just a regular guy and I guess I'm not worldly enough to know, so I ask, Do other countries have people that stupid or was this the stupidest thing that has ever been done in the history of mankind, and right here in America?

America, the land of the free, free to go where you want, free to stop when you want, free to be rich, free to be poor, free to be employed, free to be unemployed, free to be smart, free to be stupid.

Stupid In Montana As America

O yeah, let's not forget about the sixty-plus-year-olds. These idiots have been on this planet for over sixty years, and yet they are so stupid that they will stop in the middle of a public entryway and start talking to each other, completely unaware that another person might be coming along. So you have to say excuse me, and then wait for them to move their bodies out of the way so you can get by.

It reminds me of walking down a trail with cattle standing on it—you have to yell *haa, haa, look out, haa,* because they're stupid cattle and they don't know that you want to get by. But you can't call them idiots since they've only been on this planet from one to ten years or so.

But these idiot people over sixty, now that's sixty times three hundred and sixty-five, which comes to twenty-one thousand and nine hundred days they've been on this planet, and who knows how many times they've been in a public place. And yet they are still too stupid to know that another person might be coming along. I find them to be incredible.

A Piece Of Me

However, I'm always polite and just say excuse me, look the other way, and think, *Idiots, cattle mentality*, while being disgusted.

Now, I'm almost fifty years old, and I'm pretty sure the last time I was that stupid I couldn't have been more than three or four years old, but I'm sure that when I was, my mother grabbed me by the arm and yanked me out of the way and said, "Robbie, you know if you're standing in the middle of a public doorway then you will be in someone else's way."

But that was forty-six to forty-seven years ago, and I haven't been getting dumber with time. Instead I've been getting smarter, so when I'm seventy or eighty I will be smarter yet as a goal, since I believe that to go through this life as a bipedal humanoid without a brain is a real slap in the face to God.

Oh, and I'm not talking about public entries in the slums or ghettos, where those people typically need to be on their feet thinking at all times, because when you're living in the ghettos you never know when something's going to happen, so you need to be ready.

Stupid In Montana As America

I'm talking about rich people in nice places or rather, Stupid Money with Cattle Mentality, who probably arrived via Insect Mentality.

About eighteen years ago, I made some money. I was living and working in a small town in Montana called Ennis when I came across a project where we were to build a house in a place where there was one already existing. It was a beautiful property of I believe a hundred-plus acres; it was well protected from the wind since it was down in a small creek drainage with some cottonwood trees around it, and there was good grazing land on the bluffs above it.

The problem was that we needed to get the old house out of the way so we could start building the new, so I walked up to the owner

and said, "Hey, what are you going to do with this old building?"

and she said, "I don't know. We've had several of the local contractors in the area tell us to have the fire department do a fire training burn on it." That's where the fire department sets the house on fire and practices putting it out until it is burned down to the ground.

I looked at the house and pondered for about fifteen seconds and said, "Hey, I will give you ten thousand dollars for this house," and she said, "Well, you know, my father built this house and I grew up in it and I love this house, so if you want to try and save it, I will give it to you."

Well, I agreed, but it is illegal to be given real property, so I gave them a check for one dollar and a contract to move the house away, and I was the proud new owner.

So then I found a house mover to move the house, and at the same time I traded my golf course lot, which I was making payments on, with a five-acre parcel about ten miles away from the house. I built a foundation, and in two weeks time, to make a long story short, I had a property with all the amenities and a handsome amount of equity to boot, which I then used to borrow against to renovate, landscape, and build a nice big two-car garage with attached shop, and have even more value in the property.

Then I decided to sell the house, which brings me to the best part of the story.

The house was by itself amongst several thousand acres of grassland, with the exception of another house about an eighth of a mile behind it and a few more behind it yet, scattered about over a couple thousand acres.

As I said, I had landscaped, which involved planting a lawn that was about twenty-five feet wide, wrapped around three-quarters of the house. It took a lot of watering to keep it green since the house was located on the east side of the Continental Divide, and it was primarily dry country, but rich with an assortment of native grasses, which makes it good cattle country, and when I say a lot of watering, I'm talking once a day at least.

Along came a prospective buyer from Idaho. The man called me from town and arranged to meet with me on the property at a certain time.

Now, you need to realize that this man had driven north out of Idaho up Highway 287, which is driving down river, the Madison River (incidentally, one of three rivers in the nation that runs from the south to the north), approximately forty-seven miles, of which about thirty miles are grasslands with the exception of cottonwood trees lining the river. From town the man proceeded up the highway approximately another five miles to my house.

Upon his arrival, the man and I talked fairly lengthily about various issues of the house and other topics, and toward the end of the meeting he asked me about the grass. "How often do you need to water it?"

I said, "Oh, at least once a day since this is such dry country, and if you want to keep it that rich dark green color then that's what you need to do."

He replied, "No, not that grass—*that* grass," and he pointed to the native grasses on the five acres connecting to the rest of the valley.

I said, "Ha," in awe and replied with a straight face, "Oh, I don't have to water that grass, I think God takes care of that," and then quickly changed the subject.

After talking a short time further he said he would think about buying my house and get back to me later, and then he got in his car and drove off, leaving me with thinking that I, in fact, had possibly just met the stupidest person on the very face of the earth.

And I must say, I am still pondering this person to this day, and the best word I can come up with is *incredible*.

Then later I recalled him telling me about his big family of something like eight or nine kids, which brought a smug look to my face, as I thought, *Well, that's just perfect. Here's a man who's so stupid that he can't tell the difference between the native grasses that he has been driving next to for miles and miles and the domestic grass that I planted, and he is raising children. How?* I ask.

Well, he can raise them, I guess, and provide for them everything they need, except the most important thing—a brain.

These people today, I tell ya. You know, God told us to be prolific, and we are to the point that global population is a monster that's out of control and will mean the end of things as we know them, but I don't think that when God said that, he meant for us to have babies like a rabbit does.

A Piece Of Me

You know, like have as many babies as you can and then when they're weaned just set them free to fend for themselves. There's no point in teaching them anything since we don't know anything to teach anyway.

But our government doesn't care; it wants more people since more people means more tax revenue.

So the stupid keep making babies, and we just get dumber and dumber, like drones in an ant colony; at some point in the near future there will be no need to think for ourselves, and the only identity we will need is a number so we can pay our taxes.

Maybe I'm not alone in this world. Maybe there are other people out there who don't want to be part of the global population monster. Who actually have the ability to think, *Hey, since there is one-third of mankind starving to death every day, maybe instead of making a bunch of new ones we should take care of the ones we have.*

And that way living life will be more harmonious with Mother Nature instead of the scratching and clawing, fast-paced, dog-eat-dog kind of world we live in today.

Stupid In Montana As America

Yep, the average American way of thinking today is just like the average African way of thinking, and that's, well, I don't have a job, and I don't have a house, but I have a car and a dog with a car payment, and my hormones are active, and hey, I have an idea, let's have a baby and a big family just like all the animals in the animal kingdom, except when it comes to animals and their hormonal changes at times when they can't provide enough food for the table, Mother Nature kicks in and stops the influx of hormones so they don't have the desire to have babies or especially the need.

She doesn't do that for people since I guess she figures people are born with a brain so they shouldn't need instinct to tell them not to have babies when they can't even provide for themselves.

But please, don't get me wrong. I think that family is a great thing, in fact one of the greatest of things, but at the same time you only need three things to make a family, and that is a man and a woman and a child.

And in this day and age that's a smart figure as well, not eight or ten or fifteen and stupid.

A Piece Of Me

Last winter I was sitting at a traffic light when along came a man who was probably in his sixties. He was walking in a good and healthy stride with what appeared to be a destination in mind, seeing as how he was wearing a sweat suit and had sneakers on.

I noticed he pushed the crosswalk button so the light would change and he could cross the intersection safely, but the problem was that he pushed the wrong button. He pushed the button that signals the light to change for the crossing that crosses away from me and then he stood at the corner to cross in front of me, and after waiting for about one minute with the light not changing, he decided to cross anyway.

Then the light changed and he was on his way, and I thought to myself, *What an idiot*. I mean, where would you have to be from to not know how to cross a street at an intersection, and at this particular one, there's a sign, as with most, right above the button, with a big arrow pointing which way to go.

Well, maybe he's not from here; maybe he is from a place where they don't have traffic lights and this is the first one he has ever seen, and I was lucky enough to be there at that time to witness it.

But wait a minute, this guy was in his sixties. Do you mean to tell me that this guy has lived all those years and never needed to cross a street with a traffic light? Or could it be that he is just that stupid?

I know, maybe he's mentally retarded, but I doubt it; on the other hand, I guess stupidity is a form of a mental handicap, just self-inflected.

So then I started thinking, *Hey, maybe that was the grass guy,* but then no, he wasn't that tall and I didn't recognize him.

INSECT MENTALITY

Insect Mentality, all the way up the road, in a place where the author has seen a fisher, pine martin, coyotes, bear, moose, numerous deer and eagles, and awesome views.

But the only thing this moron will see is bumper.

I'm calling this scene Insect Mentality in Humans.

This highway is over one hundred miles long and yet these people are climbing over each other in a hurry to get nowhere important and late, reminding me of a trail of ants.

CHAPTER 3
Life On The Go

It's how we do it in America, in our high-speed, highly technologically advanced era, with all our stress that we only have our individual selves to blame for.

We get in our cars every day and break all the driving rules that were designed to protect us and risk our lives to get to a dead-end job, and why? Because we are too stupid to set our alarm clocks ten minutes ahead and get out of bed.

Well, not me. I've never been that stupid, but as I go down the road every day I see many who are.

Stupid In Montana As America

Four winters ago I was a snow bird and I was on my way to work on the house that the actor John Ritter grew up in, in Toluca Lake, California, which is in the LA basin.

I was doing the finish carpentry, which entailed two different styles of five-piece crown moldings throughout the whole house, and in addition numerous other moldings, which meant working with mutable angels and degrees in angles. Needless to say, this made it a real mind job.

Well, on my way to the job one day, I was in no hurry as usual, driving on the 210 freeway at a point where an onramp merged on my right, and at the same time that ramp merged onto the 210. As the part of the 210 that I was on changed into the 134, here he came, merging to the left from the onramp in a small, unibody car with a full-sized tractor-trailer attempting to merge to the right at the same time where the 210 was connecting to the 134 in the same place, and he was going about the same speed as me, which was about sixty-five miles per hour.

Now, this guy in the unibody had a couple of choices:

one, he could slow down and merge behind the tractor-trailer, or pull out to the left and take one of the five lanes that were available since it was about six-fifteen in the morning and there was hardly anybody out on the road yet.

But no, he was in a hurry, so he decided to pull in front of the tractor-trailer but didn't have enough speed or power, and as my jaw dropped, the driver laid on his horn and probably didn't even bother hitting the brakes. Meanwhile, without enough room to put a piece of paper between their two bumpers, the unibody, while fishtailing, pulled to the left to get out of the way, but there was not enough room because now there was a center divider and it was too late. He hit the center divider and went airborne, landing on the 134 Freeway and fishtailing at sixty-five miles per hour, and then miraculously he straightened it out, and I yelled to myself, *He's alive,* and laugh, and think, *What an idiot…must be an American.*

When is it going to be fast enough, you know, like if they post the speed law at seventy miles per hour, then these idiots will go eighty to ninety, and if they post it at one hundred and ten then you know they're going to go a hundred and thirty to forty. I mean, these people are just that stupid.

They don't care if they live or die or care if anyone else does either, and that's why I call them stupid, uncaring idiots.

I blame it on too many people with too many problems, so they're having to go faster and faster to get somewhere with nowhere to be, and for years it's been widely known about the rat race in the cities, but now it's in the country too.

I believe that man can and will one day be able to travel at or faster than light speed, but when he can, I hope he is smart enough to plot a course that is uninhabited with something in the way, unlike these idiots who come here to Montana from the city and have to ruin three or four of their vehicles before they realize that there are deer in the roads here.

But nothing teaches like pain, like if you fall off a ladder and you break a rib or an arm, you quickly learn next time to read the label that's on the side of every ladder all across the nation, which tells you the precise angle to position the ladder in, among other equally important things that are details I won't bore you with.

With the pain of replacing a vehicle three or four times, along with the frightening experience of slamming into a deer, you would think these idiots might learn, but they don't—they just keep on keeping on.

I had a girlfriend a few years ago who claimed she had hit five deer and said she was tired of it, as we went around an almost ninety-degree turn in the highway that the locals call Deer Corner.

So I replied, "Well, you know, at this time of day I wouldn't drive faster than fifty miles per hour through here since it's obviously a deer crossing. You know, with the line of trees adjacent to a field, at the time of day when all the deer are returning from the fields to bed down in the trees on the other side of the road."

Well, she didn't say anything and just kept driving, but was probably thinking something like, *Oh, this guy thinks he is so smart and he's a know-it-all.* Of course she wouldn't say that to my face, but if she had, I would have replied, "Well, I might not be the smartest guy in town, but I'm pretty sure I'm smarter than your average deer."

The very next day we were going through that exact same stretch of road when *bam*, at seventy miles per hour; neither one of us knew what had happened, so I looked out the passenger window, and up at the top of the trees was a deer doing a perfect gainer somersault, flying through the air completely lifeless, and as my girlfriend slowed to a stop, the deer landed alongside in the barrow pit and bounced about five feet in the air and then rolled to a stop.

And needless to say, I said, "Well, now you've gotten six."

She didn't see the humor in that, seeing as how it was her car and all, and again I might add.

That relationship wouldn't have lasted anyway, due to what I talked about earlier, bad upbringing. As I found out later, she was one of those type of gals who are out there looking for a man to get pregnant by so they can leave the man and get on child support.

I mean, when you talk about losers, I'm talking total

loser. Growing up to be just like her mother, so I was lucky, real lucky. Especially when you consider that at the same time I was working on another property development deal, from which I made a lot of money.

So that's how we do it in America—we grow up and have kids as soon as we can, before we grow a brain, because we don't know any better, and we don't know any better because our parents didn't know any better. Or in some cases we figured we would grow the brain later, which never happens since by then we are just too tired, I guess.

It amazes me that in this country our dogs have to have a license to leave the yard, and in many cases even be in the yard, so as to bring responsibility back onto us when it decides to run down the street and get into the neighbor's trash, pee in their flower garden, and mate with their dog.

And yet we don't need one for our kids, or for that matter to even have kids. We don't need to pass a basic test to show that we can do simple arithmetic or even that we can read and write; we don't need a high school diploma or to prove that we can hold down a job or any-thing at all. Basically we can have babies with the mind capacity of an insect and we are perfectly legal.

It's perfectly okay to be stupid parents as long as we provide a home and put food on the table, but in many cases these parents today can't do that since they aren't able to pass a simple test, and that is why we have wel-fare.

Montana is full of welfare recipients, and I have either known or at least known of many, maybe as many as one hundred or so, and thinking back on them, I don't think I have known any who couldn't work and hold down a job.

But they did all have one thing in common, and that was they were stupid people. So that just goes to show you that the only real qualification to be on welfare is stupidity. I'm guessing, then, that most of this country qualifies to be on welfare.

So here's an idea; let's just keep making babies and not teach them anything and eventually we will all be on welfare with no one paying taxes.

At least then the government might be inspired to

start a licensing agency that requires testing for would-be parents.

With seven billion people in the world today, our country needs to set an example for the rest of the world before it's too late.

As the Dalai Lama stated, every single being is precious, but quality of life would be better than quantity.

I, of course, didn't need him to tell me that, since I have known that for at least thirty years, and as far as change is concerned, the Bible indicates that man can change these things, but he won't.

But at the same time I believe that you have to have hope and keep on trying, which is perhaps why I am writing this book.

A couple of years ago I was frequenting my favorite lake campground and in it was another fisherman like me, but unlike me he was one of those people who just think they know it all and the rest of the world is ignorant. He also had one of those dogs that would bark and snarl at you like at any second he was going to bite, and the owner would say, "Oh, don't worry, he won't bite," and I would think, *Man, I wish I had a gun so I could shoot the dog and say, "I know."*

But every day that I was going out fishing I would typically see him, and if I acknowledged to him that I was going fishing that day, he would, one hundred per-cent of the time, go on to tell me what to use, when to use it, and where, and I would typically just listen and then say, "Oh," and then, "Thanks for that information" and be on my way, knowing all along that I have probably forgotten more about fishing on this particular lake than he will ever know.

But that's one of the symptoms of the illness, and that is the thinking that you know more than another person, so you're always telling and never listening. It's like the wise man once said, "It's the fool who chatters, while it's the wise man who listens."

So needless to say this guy never learned anything from me, and I guarantee you that I out-fished this guy in probably the first half-hour of every time I went out, hands down.

But maybe that's where it starts, you know, this guy's

probably been telling and not listening his whole life, and that's why he is, and you know what, stupid.

Forgetting about being humble and assuming that I know more than you based on nothing is the formula to stupidity.

I don't mean to promote Buddhism, but we do just the opposite of what a young Buddhist monk does in that we learn all kinds of stuff, but we don't learn thought stimulation or control of our minds. A Buddhist monk first learns the nature of his mind, then the materialistic world.

But we are not Buddhists, and thank God, but instead we are Americans and what we were doing up until thirty years ago was pretty good, but now we are falling behind in many ways, and I think it stems from the illness that we are so deeply infected with.

So what do we do? Well, I don't know, but I'm sure going to point it out so that maybe someone smarter than me will do something, since God knows, there's lots of them out there.

It seems to me that in order to solve problems we need to look to someone more intelligent and wise and ask their advice; perhaps we should elect our leaders on the same principle so they can lead us into a less problematic lifestyle.

Instead of electing the one who talks the best talk, on top of the talk, show, and dance, they have a written and oral examination at the end, and if they can pass it then we have found a new president, and yeah, we found someone who has some real answers to the problems in this country and is smart enough to apply a fix. Someone who we know is smart enough to handle the job rather someone who had enough financial backing to put on the big show and dance, so we end up with someone who isn't just a good talker but can solve problems, too.

But back to the subject at hand, stupid in America—I know that the problem is global, and I think we need to fix number one first and then we can go abroad and help others, which is the good Christian thing to do, the very foundation of this one-nation-under-God-for-which-it-stands country.

The Amazon Indians used to be the most stupid and backward people on the face of the earth but not anymore.

About twenty years ago, a friend of mine was sitting in a bar in the city of West Yellowstone, when the lady on his right, who seemed to be in her thirties, turned to him and said, "Excuse me, can you tell me how old they are when that one," pointing to the antelope mount hanging on the wall to the left side of them, "turns into that one," pointing over to the mule deer mount to the right of them.

And my friend looked at the lady, hesitated for a moment, and said, "Oh, about three years," with a straight face and obviously laughing inside, and she said, "Oh," and went on her way.

Well, needless to say, that spread through town so fast, and it spread out of town as well, and so far out of town that I've heard the story in another state. And keep in mind that West Yellowstone is a staging point for the tourists before they head into the park to mostly look at and observe animals, which costs money, so in all likeliness this person was probably not from a ghetto where her parents couldn't afford to put her through school but instead probably just the opposite.

Stupid In Montana As America

So thinking back on that story (and I do believe it's true since my friend swears up and down that it is), I once again have tried to figure out where this person could be from, and once again I can't turn to the Amazon jungle since I can't imagine an Amazon Indian who could be that stupid. I mean, it's just not possible, so if I wanted to find this person, where in the world would I go?

Well, I guess by now you've figured out that I will stay here in the states and probably my first state of choice would be California.

Yep, they've got some real doozies in that state, as they come here to Montana all the time and ask some really stupid questions. But I've got to say that that's not where all the stupid money's coming from, for it's coming from all over the nation and there seems to be no end to it.

Back in the early 1980s I was attending real estate seminars and money seminars, also one called The Psychology of Winning by Dennis Waitley, and the people who were giving these seminars in most counts were multimillionaires, and the bottom line that I personally obtained from these people was that money is attracted and not earned. Thirty years later I have found this to be quite true, even in this day and age, but it's changed to just the opposite of what it was, in that now to attract money you need to be stupid or at least act stupid.

I have difficulty doing this, and believe me I have tried; in fact, every time I find a new job working with a bunch of new people, the first thing I typically do is act as stupid as I can so as to fit in, which usually works for about two weeks, but every time after that two-week period, it just starts to show, and before long everyone is coming to me with their questions since I typically have the answers.

Which would be great in a normal world, but in today's world and in that event, the stupid contractor doesn't get to be the big contractor with the answers since in reality that wasn't what he was hired for anyway.

He was really hired because he was stupid, and stupid is attracted to stupid, so the owners liked him and they hired him to build their multimillion dollar house, because that's what they are, too—stupid.

Stupid In Montana As America

And since money is attracted, stupid money just simply likes stupid. So if you want to be a successful contractor, all you need to do is have a song and dance, and that song and dance is, be nice and stupid, and you will fit right in with the money, that is, the stupid money.

As for me, after thirty-plus years of construction, I enjoy myself while I'm working, especially on the big jobs. I pretty much laugh all day long at all the stupid shit that goes on. It is real entertainment, and at the end of the job it's always the same problems: the tile doesn't match, or the floor isn't level with the steps, or the paint doesn't match the carpet, and on and on.

And always it's the contractor's fault, for he did this and he did that. You never hear that it's the stupid owner who hired the idiot. I knew he was an idiot within seconds of meeting him, but the owner couldn't figure it out until the end of an eighteen-month project.

One of the ways I sum it up is the simple fact that the most used word in construction in this day and age is the word *idiot.*

I must use this word fifteen times a day, and it's typically aimed toward the idiot I'm working for, or the idiot who hired him—the owner.

It used to be that if you wanted to be rich, you should go to the ghetto and watch and observe how the people there act and talk, and then do just the opposite, and money will be attracted to you.

Basically if you acted stupid, like you didn't care about anything at all, then you would fit right in. But not anymore. Now if you want to fit in with the rich, you still need to act like you care about certain topics and causes, but their stupid topics and causes, and if you act stupid about them but at the same time care, you'll fit right in.

Plus you'll fit right into America, and when you go abroad they'll say, "Oh, just another dumb-ass American asking another dumb-ass question or doing something stupid."

Just this morning I was driving down the road going around a turn on the road that overlooks Flathead Lake, and I might add that the view was amazing. It's the end of May, and the rivers are flowing at flood level, and the one hundred metric tons of mud and sediment are mixing in to Flathead Lake from the Flathead River and Swan River, so you have the rich browns mixing in with the greens and dark blues, underneath a blue sky with scattered clouds. It's an awesomely spectacular view.

So then I looked down at my speedometer and saw that I was speeding at forty-one miles per hour in a thirty-five.

I let off the gas and then looked in the mirror and saw that the idiots behind me of about six cars were right on my ass in a hurry, staring at my bumper and not even noticing the view, and so I thought, *What a bunch of low-lifes*, and all of them in brand-new gas-guzzling vehicles, in a hurry to get wherever it is they're going, totally oblivious to the reason to even be in Montana.

Then I get down to Swan Lake, which involves a winding mountain road. Every year we have different bicycle club events on this road that entail literally hundreds of bicyclists riding alongside the road, or more descriptively in the middle of the road—not in the center but away from the side—but many times they are in the center, and even though these people are obviously not in a hurry, they do exercise one of the stupidest things I know, like continuing to ride in the middle of the road as they go around a blind turn on a highway that's posted at sixty miles per hour.

Now, I'm quite certain that most people who have driven a car have probably encountered a bicyclist while driving down a road as well, so assuming that most of these bicyclists drive motorized vehicles as well, then I have to also assume that they must know that the time it takes a three-thousand-pound vehicle to stop is different than the time it takes a bicycle to speed up or slow down to maneuver around the persons on their right, especially when you consider that the ride they're on isn't the French Open.

I mean, these people are doing around ten miles per hour, so when you come around a corner in the road it's like they're standing still, and you have to dynamite the brakes. This has happened many times and people talk about it all the time, and yet the bicyclists do it anyway.

Also, you must keep in mind that I personally have put thousands of miles on a bicycle on these same particular highways, and many other places as well, and I have never, ever ridden on the left side of the white line, except in the event of obstacles on the right side of it, and the amount of times that has happened wouldn't even amount to a fraction of a percentage.

So it just goes to show you that you don't need a brain to ride a bicycle; in fact, you can be extremely stupid and live in America and be on a bicycle riding on a highway.

And then you have me. I'm the guy who comes around a corner in the road on these people and hammers the brakes, almost killing one or two of these idiots (or swerving out in the oncoming lane into oncoming traffic, which I won't do), and then I speed back up and go around the idiots, at the same time rolling down my automatic passenger side window, while I yell out, "STUPID" as I go by, and then look in my rearview mirror to see them flipping me off and yelling obscenities at me as I shake my head in disbelief and roll my window back up.

So then I arrive at one of my favorite places and begin to think like a zoologist, in that, if a person was to associate the mentality level of a bicyclist driving in the middle of a highway around a turn (or for that matter anywhere on the length of any highway in the middle anywhere in this country) with an animal who is equally as stupid, what animal would it be? It wouldn't be a bear because I have seen bears cross the road a few times, and they always look both ways before they do. They, in fact, are very conscious of vehicles motoring along. Not a raven as they, too, are very conscious and aware of the dangers of being in the road for any length of time, and of course we know that insects are, since we have them stuck all over our windshields, and then it comes to me, and it's a deer.

I have seen deer walking in the middle and down the length of a highway, and dogs as well, but not all dogs, for some dogs have enough sense to stay out of the roadway.

So there you have it, a bicyclist riding down the road in the middle has the same mind capacity as a deer, or some dogs. And you know, I would just bet that here in Montana, if the bicyclist dressed in the same color as deer, there would be dead bicyclists all up and down the side of the road, just like deer, and vice versa; if deer dressed in bright colors, you would hardly ever see them dead on the side of the road.

Yes, you might think that's pathetic, bipedal humanoids with all the means of acquiring an education along with mind development, riding around on bicycles with the mind capacity of a deer. Well, so do I, but it's my opinion that even more pathetic than that are the people who have lots of money with nothing to do.

I'm talking about the people who have money but at the same time are so empty of desire or enthusiasm to have a good time that they're bored, so what do they do? They go out and buy a job of all things.

All I can say to that is it's pathetic. It's unbelievable. These people could be anywhere in the world doing some really fun stuff, but instead they want to work like the rest of us, so they buy a job and dress down so they can look the look and talk the talk and fit in with the regular folks who have to work to make ends meet and work a little overtime so as to afford to do some of the fun stuff in life. And these idiots have money without the capacity to know what to do with it…absolutely pathetic.

Now we have an element that's beyond pathetic and goes all the way to sick and wrong, and that is the fact that the white trash types are becoming socially acceptable and probably because they have money.

So what we have is money, stupid, no class, no courtesy, white trash driving around in brand-new vehicles.

Let it be known that no amount of money could seduce me into even acting like white trash. In other words, if you told me that I could have all the money I could ever need and all I would have to do is act like stupid, uneducated, lowlife white trash, then no, just no.

They say that over one hundred thousand people die every year due to alcohol-related circumstances, and that number is growing, but alcohol is a highly toxic poison, and putting a highly toxic poison in your mouth is stupid.

I have indulged in my fair share, but it seems to me that we can't blame it all on alcohol since alcohol only enhances stupidity, when who's really to blame is the big alcohol conglomerates with all their false advertising about the subject.

Just the very word *alcoholic* was probably coined by the alcohol companies or by some doctor on their payroll. So I was thinking since they can coin a phrase like that one (as any reputable doctor knows that it's imposable for the human body to become physically addicted to a highly toxic poison) then I should be able to as well, and I was thinking about stupidaholic—once you're stupid then you are always going to be.

Someone needs to file suit against them just like they have against the tobacco companies for the same reason, since there's no real difference between the two. They both produce poisons that kill.

Yes, stupidity is affecting us all, but I think that the trick is to stay on the path—the path of being a true human being, which means to improve upon oneself spiritually, mentally, and physically one's whole life, and when you fall off the path like we all do from time to time, you get back on it, and stay on it for as long as you can. Perfection is not a destination but something to aim for, or, as I said earlier, a road.

Life on the Go

Maybe it's not so much that alcohol kills but more stupidity, as everyone knows that most people are killed because they were being stupid.

Like the guy who gets drunk and climbs into a trash bin to sleep at night, and when the trash truck shows up the next morning, he gets crushed alive, or how about the guy who's riding a motorcycle without a helmet and is speeding. Now, there's a real brainiac.

Yeah, when you think about it that way, stupidity might be one of the top killers in the world, or rather stupidism.

In the Swan

CHAPTER 4
Money Without Mind

This illness called stupidity, could it be that it has found a way to the top? I mean the very top, commander and chief of the most powerful military on the planet. If you take the one thing that stands out the most in the presidential campaign of George W. Bush, the Iraq War, and then place a word best describing his chance to have a great ally with one of the top oil producers in the world, that would be BOTCHED, and why? Personally I believe that the reason is because he failed to act upon or, rather, really act as commander and chief when the looting began to occur and thus destruction of the cities and the country as a whole.

Stupid In Montana As America

Was it possibly because the prophecies of the Bible have an uncanny way of coming to pass? Frankly, I find it hard to believe that someone who could be voted in by the populous as commander and chief could not know that to ultimately win this type of war, where we are freeing a people from oppression of an evil tyrant, you need to win over the hearts and minds of the people, and that nobody could be so stupid as to think that you're going to win over the hearts and minds of the people while you're in occupation and at the same time you've allowed their country to be destroyed.

Or perhaps there's a hidden reason for his actions, or rather lack of actions, that we don't know about, maybe something to do with the oil since obviously if you allow the second largest oil producer in the world to be destroyed, the demand of oil is going to be greater than the supply, and the price is going to go up, and possibly plunder this nation into a recession.

It makes me wonder whose side this guy is on. They're talking a projected price of the war at 1.8 trillion dollars to get rid of an idiot dictator, when for just one million we could have hired and trained one of the Iraqi snipers to kill him with a bullet... I could have paid for the bullet myself.

One thing is for sure, he wasn't on the side of the over six hundred thousand Iraqi civilians who have died so far, not to mention the countless millions who have suffered. Or for that matter the millions of us who are suffering now at the gas pump.

The war has done nothing for the security of this country; in fact, it's had just the opposite effect in that it's given the terrorists a place to learn our weaponry and how we fight, thus giving them firsthand training.

So I guess I can be stupid, too, since I voted for the guy, but on the other hand remembering back, I recollect that he was the best thing going, so on that note, I guess it just goes to show you that sometimes the best just isn't good enough.

But it's one of my beliefs that there's always hope, for without hope, mankind probably wouldn't have got past Adam and Eve.

And I don't want to get into politics too deep, especially since the last story pretty much says it all anyway.

Plus it seems as though to fix the top end of this country we need to start at the bottom and work our way up, and it strikes me that for the last twenty to thirty years it's been (primarily in this country) only the stupid ones having the babies, and that is why we have all these stupid young people running around.

Basically their parents were stupid, so the young couldn't learn anything from them since they didn't know anything or have anything to teach.

It's like Miss Gump taught Forrest, that stupid is as stupid does, and I think she might be one of the wisest women in the country since you see it everywhere you go.

But when it comes to women, I lived in the city before I lived in the country, and what I have noticed is that city women are much more intelligent than country women, generally speaking.

Perhaps it's because country women are sheltered from the big newspapers or the world news as a whole, I don't know, but I have noticed that in the city, women typically are more interested in establishing a financial way of life first, before they have a family, as opposed to women who have been raised in the country and are typically turning into grandmas by the time they're thirty-six. I suppose it's true for the men as well, but I just haven't noticed.

I also have noticed that country folk are generally more honest people with better upbringing that way, so perhaps it's all the money in the big cities that's the root of the problem.

Or perhaps it's money itself, in that it just ruins us as soon as we have it. We have all certainly seen it where you take a perfectly decent, honest, hardworking, family-oriented person who may or may not have an education and give them a pile of money and in no time at all, they turn into a drug-using piece of shit at the bottom, with no hope in sight.

Perhaps it's because when you have more money than you need and you don't give it or use it to buy food for the starving children in the world, or for thy neighbor in need, you are not spiritually correct, so the temptations of evil outweigh the good, and you become a piece of shit.

If that is the case then I don't ever want to have money that I just don't need; on the other hand I know that I could not have money that I didn't need while children were starving to death, especially in the same country, city, or, even more so, town.

Pardon me for getting away from the subject at hand, but I felt compelled to share an experience that I had today while it is fresh in my mind.

I was driving down to Swan Lake on the only road that goes there, which I have already described earlier in this book as the winding mountain road that goes on for miles with a double yellow line, when as usual while doing the speed limit of sixty miles per hour, two vehicles came on my ass, and as usual I slowed down. Then the one, upon slowing, demonstrated a thought process and passed me.

So on completion of his pass, I began to speed up when the next vehicle began to climb on my ass, so again, I began to slow down and he backed off, demonstrating thought process as well, so I naturally sped back up, and the three of us drove down the road with safe distances between ourselves as though we all had a brain, and knowing that there's plenty of highway for all of us.

So then I pondered…there is hope…even though this is the first time that I can remember three people in close proximity to each other who each demonstrated that they had a brain, so for that I am baffled, or maybe I'm in shock.

Pondering further, though, I've come to the conclusion that since I have driven that road just about every day for eleven years, which comes to just over four thousand times; minus mutable vacations and just being away I think it's safe to say around three thousand times, which makes this event around one percent of the time, which means that ninety-nine percent of the drivers in this area are idiots.

And since this type of driving doesn't come from Montana but virtually everywhere else, then it's safe to say that ninety-nine percent of the people of this country are idiots, which is interesting since this has been my guess, without doing the math, for quite some time. In fact, I have said many times over many years that I am in the one percent category of drivers in this country.

Back to the subject at hand, I was thinking that perhaps these three people drove like normal, concerned adults with a brain because that's what they were, normal people, but with a brain.

On the other hand, what is normal? I mean, in the winter when I live in Kalispell, Montana, I typically have to drive south down Highway 93, and at the south end of town there is a traffic light that is approximately one mile ahead of another light, and it's around a turn so you can't see it, but before the turn they have a flashing yellow light that tells you when the light is either yellow or red so you can time the light, which is smart, as that saves on gas and wear and tear on your vehicle. It is a four-lane stretch of highway with a left turn lane on the whole section of road.

Now, would you believe that ninety-nine percent of all the drivers I see every morning don't make that light, but instead they climb all over my ass and each other's and get around only to go as fast as they can to catch that light? Then when the light changes they all go as fast as they can to get to the next light. Every single time I typically come rolling in right behind them and barely have to slow down at all; in fact, if all those idiots weren't sitting at the light when it changed, I wouldn't have to slow down at all since I have never, ever caught that light and probably never will, as I have a brain.

It's like someone opens a gate for a bunch of hungry sheep that don't know anything else but that they are hungry and straight ahead is the food, and yes, that is normal if you're a bunch of stupid, idiot sheep.

So perhaps there's a solution to this problem that's at epidemic proportions with a government that doesn't show concern, but demonstrates just the opposite by growing bigger and bigger and allowing the school system to shrink smaller and weaker.

Perhaps if the government did just one thing, like make this book mandatory reading, and/or reading material like it, for each and every person in this country who is over the age of eighteen, that at least would have a small impact on the people, or maybe I'm just being arrogant. At any rate I would like to think that I'm being hopeful.

There's also an identity crisis that's occupying a large number of the people, and I'm sorry but it's stupid, too, like a lot of these bikers we have today.

You know, it's perfectly okay to ride a Harley Davidson while wearing normal clothing, like a pair of work boots, Levi's pants, and maybe a leather coat for protection. You don't have to buy the full biker look, and it's okay to shave as well. Like me, for example, I have owned three motorcycles, and I have ridden all over the western United States, and I never felt the need to grow a beard and basically look the look.

I guess I was just okay with myself while having a great time riding.

But it's not just the bikers, it's also the people who are skiing or bicycling or golfing, fly fishing, archery, you name it.

Fly fishermen are my favorite—it's like they just stepped right out of Cabela's magazine, and they even pose for you as you drive by, like look at me, I look just like everyone else out here who's doing this.

Money Without Mind

It's like they have been cast out of a mold and stamped with a title, this is what I am, at least until they get off of their vacation and go back to who they really are.

It's like they're almost unconscious of it since it's so much of a trend, and for some reason the coat that's been keeping them warm all winter long will not work on the river, so they feel the need to buy a Patagonia, as if the fish care.

Well, I'm here to tell you that the fish don't care, as I usually wear something that's comfortable, and I typically out fish them all.

There's definitely a level of intelligence that goes with the identity crisis thing since some of the more intelligent bikers I have met have been the real ones, who have been bikers for years and have chosen that way of life for their own reason, whatever it may be, as opposed to the Weekend Warriors.

It's also interesting how the stupid get mixed up with the crazy.

All my life I have heard people say, "That guy is

crazy," but when I interview and analyze him, I find him to be just stupid, since it's not smart to be crazy in this day and age, and it's well known that the truly crazy people are usually highly intelligent.

So when you fix the stupid problem, you are also fixing a large part of the crazy problem as well.

I'll tell you another problem that's even bigger yet, and it is the stupid insurance problem. Yep, insurance has been taking advantage of our stupidity for years.

So now it's at the point that it's just stupid that we have to have insurance for everything we do; even our dogs can have insurance, and it won't surprise me one bit when it comes to us having to have doggy insurance by law.

But it isn't just the fact that you have to have it—it's that these insurance companies are dictating how we do things to the point that they're changing the very way we live and operate through life, and I'll tell you, it disgusts me.

Especially in the business of construction, where before you even start to build, the engineer has to multiply his structural engineering figures by eighty percent in order for his insurance company to okay the project (that is, if he wants to keep his insurance) and then after everybody else's insurance checks out, you can begin to build with a bunch of junk tools that are made that way due to all the safety requirements imposed by the insurance companies. I mean, it's really bad when I have tools that are thirty years old and superior to anything that can be bought today. In fact, when I bid a project these days I have to figure in a certain percentage for buying new tools, since they just aren't going to last through the project, unless of course they are my old ones, as they will probably last another thirty years, no thanks to the insurance companies.

You know, it just occurred to me that if someone from my insurance company reads this book they're probably going to raise my rates, and they'll base it on something they'll just make up, as usual.

You know the deal, they'll just write up what they want to change in the law and give our Congressman some money and he will see to it.

We need a leader who stands up and says, "No more

special interest lobbyists. In fact, they are not even allowed in the White House, and they are a thing of the
past." And there's one campaigning on that principle
right now, but I'll believe it when I see it, since I guess
I've been lied to just too many times.

Then you have the police; as far as I know they're all
on the take.

For the last twenty years, every cop I have met will
write a no-insurance ticket, and as far as I'm concerned if
they write a no-insurance ticket then they work for organ-
ized crime since that's who is in control of insurance and
legislature.

Except for the cop I met twenty years ago who pulled
me over and asked me if I had insurance, and after I said
no, he went on to say, "Well, the insurance companies
bought legislature, so I'm not going to enforce that law."

And thinking on that later, I've come to the conclusion that he might be the only real cop I have ever met. I
mean, wow, he was a real American, and people like him
who act and not just talk make me feel proud to be an
American, damn proud.

Money Without Mind

Which brings me to an idea I've had about a militia that shows up in the event of a situation where an American is about to have his or her Constitutional rights violated. They show up in numbers as a nonviolent, peacekeeping force named We The People, and they represent a nation under God. Not as a force against but as assistance.

But that's just an idea and the problem is that it would be a full-time job, which needs to pay something like presidential wages.

We need smart leadership, but how do we vote in smart leadership when the average American operates like a stupid sheep?

Which reminds me of a story from a guy I was working with last year.

It was a Monday morning and I asked, "So, what did you do this weekend?"

He said, "Oh, I went hunting for muleys up Jewel Basin like I said I was going to do on Friday."

"Did you get one?"

"No, but I ran into this idiot up there, and I immediately started to think, *Man, this guy is really callous.*"

So I said, "Why? Was he an idiot?"

And he said, "Because we were all the way at the top of the mountain, and this guy comes up to me and says he's lost as he pulls out his map and he shows me the trail he came up, you know, at that first trailhead where you can park your car in that first turnout area."

I said, "Not at the very bottom where the road first starts to climb up the mountain. That's a good ride for horses."

He said, "Yeah."

"Wow, that would add another seven or eight miles onto his trip."

He said, "At least. And the guy goes on to ask me if there's a shorter way to get off this mountain, and I said yeah, you can just go down this trail the way I came up, and that's only about a mile to where you can park your car. Maybe someone will give you a lift down the rest of the way."

I said, "Wow, what an idiot."

"Yeah, apparently this guy wasn't smart enough to

keep driving on the road and then didn't look at his map until he got near the top.

"Then, as it turns out, this guy went on to ask if there were many bears in the area, and he exclaimed that he hadn't brought a weapon or any pepper spray, so I told him, 'Yeah, there are lots of bears here. In fact, there are supposed to be more bears per square mile right here along the Swan Range than any other place in the nation except in Alaska when the salmon are running,' and when I told him that, he got this real pale look on his face and said, 'Oh,' so I chuckled and said, 'Good luck.'"

I said, "Well, maybe he got his ass chewed and there's one less idiot in the world."

The truth of the matter is that if a predatory bear saw this guy clumsily walking down the trail like a stupid sheep and decided to chew his ass off, a few days later after the person was reported missing and they found his remains, the authorities would have to kill the bear since that is their policy. But it wouldn't be the bear's fault as he would be acting on instinct, you know, the natural process of selection, which is the predation of the weaker in the herd.

And in this case the bear would sense the weak mind and attack, and my response would be, hell, the bear probably thought he was doing us a favor, leave him alone.

I feel the need to share with you that just now I was writing the last paragraph here in the Swan Range outside, in my plastic chair with my feet up on a grassy bank about three feet from the creek, in my backyard on an awesomely beautiful day with all the beautiful vegetation of paper birch trees mixed with aspens, cottonwoods, and spruce pines, and the birds singing.

Yeah, it's my little piece of heaven.

So I was sitting there writing when I felt like something was watching me. I looked up and directly on the other side at about fifteen feet was a mule deer doe standing there watching me, and when she saw me look up at her, she ran about ten yards and stopped and listened to hear if I was chasing, and then she quietly moved off.

Money Without Mind

I love this place.

And as far as all the idiots around here are concerned, they may be stupid, but they are smart enough to be here.

The author with a huge pike he caught on an
artificial lure that he built in May of 2005.

The author's little piece of heaven

CHAPTER 5
All In A Day

Here in Montana we may have a similar situation as New Orleans, in that we have lots of people building in flood plains.

Even after Hurricane Katrina, we have thousands and thousands of people building their homes in places that have been completely under water in the past, and more than once, and not that long ago.

Well, that's just stupid, and I know all the justifications to it, and it's still just stupid. It's like my dad said many years ago: God gave man a mind so that he could be smart enough to not build his house in a flood plain— that way when the weather recycles to a high-water season, his house doesn't get washed away.

Stupid In Montana As America

Yet in this day and age, that's exactly what we are seeing. Many are buying houses already built in large subdivisions unbeknownst and un-warned that the entire area their little house is built on is what geologists call alluvial deposited sedimentary material, meaning the dirt was brought in from the mountains above by way of massive flooding.

But they're not the ones who really interest me, as they're mostly the younger people just trying to make their way in life, all caught up in their bills and kids, hormones and mess.

For me it's the multimillionaires who are building their humongous houses next to big rivers on the fifty-year flood plain. These are the ones, as they somehow are intelligent enough to have the money and hang onto it and yet do something so stupid that (according to some archeological findings) even primitive man wouldn't do.

Actually I believe that if a beaver (which is among the rodent family) lived as long as we do, it wouldn't be so stupid, either.

So when their houses begin to wash away, and some

already have, they can bring in the sand bags and the tractors and work through the night in the rain.

So why is it that I can walk along a river or in a valley and know where the high-water line is? Well, because I have studied some basic geology, and I'm smart enough to go to the library and look up the area's history, or, in short, because I have a brain.

Here's something I would like to know. Why don't these people get fined by the government when the river destroys their house and carries all the debris into the river system? You see it on the news where a whole house has broken in half and fallen into the river or lake system, and the owners are on the news (and that's national news) saying, "Oh, we are really sad, but insurance is going to pay for it, and maybe someday we will build again." You never hear about the fines. I mean, it's stupid—these people have just dumped an equivalent of something like five years of trash in the bio aqua system and yet they are exempt from penalty for being incredibly stupid because they are having tough times.

It was bad enough that they built that great big house

right next to the river, which was obtrusive as hell to all the people who had been floating it, but you know, I'm not exactly Mr. Happy when I get my fishing lure snagged on their couch at the bottom.

I think they should have to clean all that crap up.

And then we have the ones who build their house in a place that's consistently struck by lightning and wind-swept so severely that nothing has grown there for thousands of years, and they can't figure out why their garden won't grow well.

Yet with all the stupid money they can afford to build a house.

You know, I've never thought of myself as a genius, but it seems to me that if I was going to build a house in a place like along the shoreline of Florida where hurricanes have been frequenting for thousands if not millions of years, I would build one that is octagonal in shape so as to make it aero- and hydrodynamic. I would build it out of concrete, with bulletproof glass and metal doors and a roof with strong ties that go from the roof down through the walls into the foundation, for not very much more money.

All In A Day

Yep, I could build a house that could withstand thousand-mile-per-hour winds, but it would still be hard to get flood insurance, and of course it wouldn't have the look of the area, but who cares about that. If you're going to build, then build smart or don't build at all and find another place to build your flimsy house, somewhere where there isn't much weather, like the desert.

Then you have the ones who come to Montana with the thinking that if they have it in four-wheel drive they can go faster on the ice. Well, that's the same mind capacity that primitive man was using when he first invented the wheel, so from that alone I have come to the conclusion that man has not progressed much in mind expansion since the beginning.

We've just acquired more information, and that is why we keep doing stupid shit like crashing into another boat in the middle of a lake.

I mean, how do you do that? Well, I guess if you push the throttle all the way open and concentrate really hard so as to clear your mind of all thought, oh, and close your eyes, that's very important, and then wait until you hear a really loud noise.

And I hope some idiot doesn't read this and try this technique as it will surely work, and I know there are people out there who are just that stupid, so please don't try this at home.

But you know, we've all done stupid shit, and I am not exempt, but the difference with me is that I strive for improvement when there are so many who don't. They don't just do stupid—they are stupid.

It reminds me of the time I was driving down the Swan Highway on my way to work about ten years ago when I came upon a vehicle's lights that were heading in the opposite direction but were off the road, and one was pointed upward toward the tree tops in a stopped position.

It was about a half hour before sunrise when all the deer are out crossing the road. Now personally when I'm driving at that time of night and especially on that particular highway (since that highway at that time of night is one of the most dangerous I know of) I tend to not go faster than fifty miles per hour because any faster is suicide. There are a lot of deer crossing.

All In A Day

But she was off the road after hitting a deer at probably over seventy miles per hour (since her full-sized car was totaled) and walking around in shock asking for glasses, so I, being a good Samaritan, began to search, and as I entered the driver's side door I placed my left hand on the exploded air bag and all the dry chemical inside came gushing out into my face, which needless to say ruined my day as I was inhaling at the same time, but live and learn.

Today it happened again, the bear thing I mean. I was going to work southbound on the East Shore Highway along Flathead Lake at fifty miles per hour since that is the speed limit, and I was in no hurry as usual, when some idiot climbed on my ass. So as usual I slowed to forty and then he got closer as he was totally incapable of figuring out why. About two hundred yards ahead of us, a nice big black bear crossed. So I slowed even more to see the bear and looked in my mirror and saw that the idiot behind me didn't see it, so I laughed and took it back up to forty.

Then on my way home I stopped at the local mini

mart and there were some bicyclists there so I said, "Hey, you guys are just the ones I've been looking for" and one of them said, "Oh, why is that?" and I said, "Because right now I am writing a book, and one of the things in it is about bicycling in Montana, and I was wondering about the bicyclists who ride side by side around a turn and don't have a mirror to see the cars that are approaching from behind. One of the bicyclists stated that he had a mirror on his bike, but the ones who don't are people who just don't care and think that they will live forever and ever. I said, "Ha, well, thanks for your time," and he said, "You're welcome."

So I walked away and thought, *Well, that's just perfect and just what I thought, STUPID, but all in a day.*

Speaking of stupid, I've been reminded of all the times I have had to wait for these idiots who come here to Montana on vacation and drive through our two-lane towns and window shop from their vehicles. Yeah, it's unbelievable, they are either too lazy, too old, too fat, or just too stupid to park their vehicle and walk through a town that's only a couple of city blocks in length, and then they wonder why we hate them.

I tell you, these people in the wintertime and in the south are called snowbirds, and up here in the summer they're called tourists, and they must be the most hated people in the nation, simply because they drive too slow through our towns.

I've seen it where they've had a quarter of a mile of traffic backed up behind them while they occupy the only road through town, to window shop.

But we do like their money; we just don't want the stupid that goes with it.

You know, I would like to send them all a personal reminder every year before they leave home, and in essence it would say, "Now, this year when you pack all your things and leave for your destination, don't forget to bring your brain as well," short and sweet.

Then you have these people who just can't do the speed limit for whatever reason, and you know, I don't have a problem with that, as I will do a correct and well-mannered pass as I always do.

But when they have fifty vehicles behind them and are

too stupid to pull over, then we have a problem. That is why we have laws, like when there are more than five vehicles behind you, you have to pull over by law, but these idiots don't know shit like that. They're just driving somewhere.

And then you have these people who are towing a boat on the way to the lake. Now, I'm talking about a three-thousand-pound boat behind a thirty-eight-hundred-pound truck in a hurry at seventy miles per hour in a sixty mile per hour zone, to go fishing.

So when they get there, it's throw your shit in the boat and launch since the fish don't wait. But in reality, the fish aren't going to be even interested in feeding for three more hours. So these idiots risked their lives and everyone else's to get somewhere on time.

I see it almost every day, where one of these idiots will go past me in the opposite direction at seventy or eighty miles per hour to try and outsmart a fish that had them outsmarted from the get go.

But then, what was I thinking? I mean, the fish have a brain.

All In A Day

A couple of days ago another motorcyclist died on the lake road. Apparently he was riding on a twenty-thousand-dollar bike with a bald tire on the front at thirty-five years old. Incredible.

Well, I don't know everything, but I do know that life is worth a little bit more than a one-hundred-and-fifty-dollar tire; in fact, one of the first things I learned about riding a motorcycle is to make sure that you always have really good tires since that's the only thing between you and the road.

On previous page is the author's niece with a nice pike that she caught all by herself on an artificial lure that her dad built.

They say that you get a lot of your aunt and uncle's genes, so I was thinking maybe someday she will be a world-class fisherman and write a book like her uncle.

CHAPTER 6
Mountain Stupid To Boot

For Fme fishing and hunting are my two faveret-favorite things to do, but I gotta tell yayou, that theirsthere are more and more people doing it.

And with the hordes of people come the idiots.

Just last year I was hiking along in the woods with my 243 Seiko when I saw two people in their blaze orange hunting vests paralleling alongside of me, as I sort of popped out on a little rise, and at the same time I could see that it was a father and son team, with the son being in his early teens. Right then they saw me, and the son pulled up his rifle to see me better through his scope.

Stupid In Montana As America

I premeditatedly had put a large tree between us and saw his dad grab the rifle and push it down.

Now, I know if he had been paying attention in the hunter safety course, he would have learned to never use your scope to identify game, and somehow he passed the test, but it's probably his dad's fault for not reviewing these things before the hunt.

Perhaps his dad doesn't know any better, so he couldn't recite good safety precautions to the kid. At any rate it was a stupid move, and it's these kinds of things that make it hard to be out there anymore without being a little scared.

Yeah, these days there is so much stupidity out there that a person can't be too cautious, and it's a real rock and a hard place for me since I love to hunt, but at the same time, I know that there are people out there with a high-powered rifle in their hands walking around on two feet without a brain.

And nowadays, there is a new trend of hunters who, I'm sorry to say, aren't out there for the meat but to drink beer and kill something with horns so they can show off the horns, I guess.

Yep, these zeros will spend thousands of dollars to hike around in the woods and shoot shit and never even take an interest in learning how to cook it. They really disgust me.

I think they're all a bunch of lowlifes, and I wouldn't wipe my ass on any of them, not to hold back or anything.

Hunting is supposed to be a gentle sport with a connection between the hunter and the game and respect for all of God's creatures, but these slobs are ruining it for all of us with their actions and their powder pig stories.

Mostly because they get the ignorant anti hunters who have power in high places changing or, worse yet, managing our hunting and fishing, as they are the ones who do the most damage to the wildlife, with the reintroduction of the wolves being the best example, and the stopping of the mountain lion hunting in California being another. Now the deer herd is so weak that the lions are preying on dogs, cats, and even people, which would never happen if the lions' numbers were kept in check with game management.

It's gotten to the point where I don't even want to hunt in this country anymore, but it doesn't make a lot of sense to do the basic hunting in another country since if you start spending a lot of money to acquire meat then you are doing it for the wrong reasons, and by basic hunting I mean table fare.

Yep, fishing and hunting should be a memorable and enjoyable experience where there are no times when a guy gets angry at an idiot, but things have changed.

Two years ago I was hunting for elk with my bow and I found one—he wasn't huge or anything, but he was a nice bull, and I decided to try for him.

I had seen him through the binoculars from afar, and he was way down in this drainage where I had to scale a death-defying landslide and cross a treacherous waterfall only to hike about two miles upstream and set up, when I heard an idiot do an elk bugle.

I knew he was an idiot because he was about a mile away at the top, on a road end, and I could hear his dog barking back at his truck at the same time.

Mountain Stupid To Boot

So all was for nothing since elk aren't stupid, and certainly not stupid enough to be fooled by an idiot like that, so needless to say, it was over and I had to hike all the way back out of there pissed off.

It used to be that if you hiked in a fair distance you could get away from people, but not anymore, with all their access to llamas and horses and equipment like four-wheelers and motorbikes, people are just getting everywhere these days.

It wouldn't surprise me one bit to see someone spending thousands of dollars and parachuting in, risking their lives parachuting into trees to boot.

But I try not to get angry; instead I think about my closeness with God and Mother Nature, take in a deep breath, and continue to enjoy just being there. Money can buy my way of life, but not from me, as it's not for sale.

Yeah, if there are people doing it, then you can bet they're stupid too, so with this new age of people, those two go hand in hand.

And I couldn't even begin to go into what happens when you mix alcohol with stupid, for that's a book in itself. But that's exactly what you have when you have stupid people in the mountains, but not always; in fact, more often than not, it's the other way around, and those are the ones I'm going to concentrate on since they're the most interesting, I mean stupid without alcohol, just stupid.

I mean, it's always been fun making fun of them, but nowadays it's getting to be such a problem with the stupid events increasingly occurring in frequency and intensity, and it's just not funny anymore.

And don't get me wrong; it's not just the people coming into Montana but the ones who are from here, which tells me that it's contagious.

For example, there were a couple of guys a few years ago who shot and killed a llama, tagged it, and then dressed it out, loaded it into their truck, and took it to the butcher as an elk.

Far be it from me to say, but I grew up in California and I knew the difference between a llama and an elk when I was a small child, and these guys were adults from here where elk live. I mean, they went to school here and ate breakfast, lunch, and dinner and maybe even worked on a ranch. I'm sorry but I just can't comprehend that one.

One thing for sure is that growing up in Montana isn't enough. You better have something more going for you than just being from here, and those two guys are proof of that.

Of course I didn't need any proof since I acquired all the proof I needed when I first came here. But it used to be, back in the day, that if some idiot came to town and drove like an idiot, it wouldn't be long before the local sheriff would either get them to stop or run them out of town. But not anymore, since nowadays there are so many of them that the police can't keep up. I mean, they're everywhere. When I go to town anymore I don't just see one or two, I see most of the people around here driving like assholes.

They have no common courtesy, no manners, no respect, and in short they drive like a piece of shit, and I have it figured out since I have been watching them for several years now.

Stupid In Montana As America

Yep, I often will follow them and see how they park, get out and walk through people, etc. as I observe and analyze. And I have come to the conclusion that if you drive like a piece of shit, it's because that's what you are, and if you drive like a stupid idiot, it's because that's what you are.

They used to drive the same way down in the LA area about twenty years ago, until people started getting shot, and that changed things, and even to this day you don't see that kind of low-class type of driving down there; instead, people have manners or at least show them.

So I think that's what it's going to take, and I guess you would call it vigilante justice, but down in LA only a few people had to die, whereas all the hundreds of thousands and possibly millions of dollars spent on the police force didn't even compare to what just a few bullets did.

And personally I don't want anyone to die, but I fear it won't be long since these assholes just can't stop— that's not just how they are, but what they are.

But don't get me wrong, not everyone around here is an asshole. I see the good ones, too; unfortunately it's just not that often, but more often than not it's the ones in the less expensive vehicles.

I just had an interesting experience at the local market that I would like to share, now that I have stopped at one of my favorite places where I like to write.

I went in to buy some things for dinner, carrying my reusable shopping bag, when I came to the end of an aisle, and there were two ladies, both of whom looked like they were ten to fifteen years younger than me, so somewhere in their early forties to late thirties, with shopping carts pointed in opposite directions, talking to each other with their two young kids standing next to them.

I looked up and saw that there was no way to get by, and immediately thought to myself, *STUPID*, and at the same time one of the kids looked at me with an *I'm sorry* look on his face. Luckily there was a side aisle to the left, so I turned and went down it, which was a detour of about ninety feet, and I did this instead of saying excuse me, because I figured it would take a lot less calories overall than it would have for them to move their big fat asses out of the way, and a lot faster too.

And then I grabbed some sausage and turned to the butcher lady and said to her, "I'm writing a book right now about stupid people in Montana and the nation, and situations like that right there (as I pointed to the ladies in the aisle) are in it and I didn't bother saying excuse me since I figured it was easier for us all for me to just go around. Goddamn."

And she laughed

I said, "See, you laughed and that is good, since I'm wording it in the same way that I normally talk, so you will probably like it."

I moved off to do more shopping, but not down that aisle since the ladies were still standing there talking, totally oblivious to their surroundings. I don't think they ever knew that I had to go around them, or maybe they did but didn't care, but then that would make them not ladies, but something else, so I'll just leave it at that.

And then you have the stupidest person in recorded park history.

It was in Yellowstone Park and according to the park

this man reached out in front of a dozen or so other spectators, and touched a sow grizzly bear as she was feeding on grass with a cub next to the road. Obviously she and her cub were quite accustomed to people, and luckily they ran away.

Apparently it was a bear that primarily fed on elk calves during the spring in the calving grounds where the incident occurred, and as soon as the park rangers heard about the incident they started a massive search with a description of the vehicle and persons, but it was a government operation and the person was never found.

So let's clarify our understanding of this person. Now, you have in the world the African lion, the Siberian tiger, and the grizzly bear as the three top most powerful predators in the mammalian family of today, not counting the killer whale or the polar bear or giant squid since they live in completely different realms away from civilization.

And this person reached out and touched one, with obviously no respect or understanding of this fact. So where could this person come from in the world and not know any better? Could he be from a remote tribe of Indians in the Amazon jungle that has had no contact with the outside world, ever?

But wait, he was driving a vehicle with an American license plate.

Personally I would love to find this person so I could study and analyze him and document my findings for future reference.

I would find things out like, can he read and write, does he know what a television is, has he ever heard of world news, does he know that the world is round, does he know that the moon and stars are not just a big painting someone hung up in the sky?

I mean wow, that story is incredible, as he might have been, in fact, the absolute stupidest person on the very face of the earth.

But then again I'm reminded of one of the most definitely stupid people I have ever met in Montana.

It was nineteen years ago back in 1989 at a video store, where you would think that in the video business, the employees would be at least slightly aware of what goes on in the world.

So I walked in and looked around for a little bit and said, "Do you have any Bruce Lee movies?" and the clerk said, "Who is that?" and I said, "Ha. Do you know who Bill Clinton is?" and she said, "Yeah, he's the president."

I thought, *Wow, she knows who Bill Clinton is but not Bruce.* Well, she must be from Montana, and hopefully she doesn't go anywhere else in the world. I mean, what an idiot.

One of several places where the author writes.

CHAPTER 7
Their Planet

I t's not our planet. I mean, it was, if you believe in God and that man was made in His image and woman was made from the rib of man.

But God told us to be good to the Earth, and we have ignored that, along with most all of his other laws, and now we're facing some real problems because of it, with Global Pollution, Global Warming, and the Population Monster looming over us and encroaching at our back door.

It would be our planet if we existed with all of Mother Nature's abundance of life with peace, harmony, and love, but we don't; instead we do just the opposite in just about everything we do.

Stupid In Montana As America

Mother Nature keeps trying to intervene with disease, famine, and war among other things, but man prevails and keeps on prevailing.

Man should start working on the positive things instead of prevailing over the negatives that Mother Nature keeps throwing at us.

For example, take the houses that we live in—if instead of trying to impress the Johnsons with the beautiful wood siding, the white picket fence, and lawn, but rather we all lived in moderately sized earth homes that were underground with only a large south-facing low E window exposed at the surface, and fiber optics skylights that illuminated the house better than most houses today, and on top of that we all drove smart, compact hybrid vehicles, we would not have an energy crisis looming over us but instead a surplus of energy that we could manage for all.

But that is an extremity and to even grasp such a concept, one needs to place one's mind somewhere way off into the future, so back to reality. We find ourselves with some of the simple problems that would be easy to fix if we could just find someone who could take charge and say something like, "Hey, it's stupid to have fifteen hundred wolves in the Yellowstone ecosystem eating up all the deer and elk that we hunters paid for every time we bought a hunting license, I mean paid to expand their population."

We need a reasonable number of wolves, like say, three hundred, which would only kill as few as sixty elk per week or somewhere around one hundred and fifty deer per week so that the PETA people and all the other animal-loving types can still enjoy watching wolves brutally rip apart and eat live baby elk as they scream for their lives.

It's really not that complicated, and as an archery hunter I personally have a lot of respect for these animals, so it's heartbreaking for me to see a wolf kill an elk, especially a big bull elk, as they do not discriminate; they just kill and eat and waste, and they will keep wasting until the predator-to-prey ratio is correct.

It's basic biology to know that in all ecosystems you have a thing called predator-to-prey ratios, and since in this ecosystem we have man, who has encroached in on the system with his housing and all his developments, we must have management of the ecosystem like we did before, with game management, which was paid for by us hunters. And now that the ignorant animal lovers have intervened with the implantation of the wolves, they need to understand that the elk and the deer are a much more valuable resource than the wolves are.

But don't get me wrong, I think that wolves are a beautiful animal as all animals are. In fact, I had a wolf trotting fifteen yards in front of my vehicle at fifteen to twenty miles per hour down a dirt road for a whole mile about four years ago, and I've got to tell you it was an experience I will never forget. I mean, it was awesome, but my experiences with elk have been much more awesome and rewarding to boot.

So if you're someone with a brain and you're out hunting and you come across a wolf, just remember one thing: you have the legal right to shoot it if you feel threatened and you stick to that story.

It's the same thing with the salmon. We're talking

about hundreds of billions of pounds of fish that are lost due to the lack of fish ladders around the dams in Oregon, Washington, and Idaho, which the energy companies say would cost too much. They say they would cost hundreds of millions of dollars, when I could build one hell of a fish ladder for just four or five million.

So we pay our politicians big money and nothing ever gets done, but I think some tremendous change is in the making and is going to happen soon.

It seems as though just about everyone I talk to is aware of the Stupid Crisis that is plaguing our nation, and I wonder why that is. Could it be that I only talk with at least semi-intelligent people, or have I just been lucky?

At any rate I believe that in the end, Mother Nature will prevail and we will succumb to her, and in that time we will be faced with coexisting with their planet with peace, harmony, love, and knowledge as to make it our planet.

Lawrence E. Joseph, author of *Apocalypse 2012*, theorized that volcanoes erupting more frequently could be Mother Nature's way of combating global warming, in that volcanoes place tons of ash into the upper atmosphere and block the sun, which cools down the planet, along with hurricanes, mud slides and ultimately mega disasters that kill humans who are responsible for the greenhouse gasses causing the warming trend.

Personally I believe this to be true, and as I stated earlier I believe she's even using war, because there are just too many people.

And perhaps she is the one responsible for the stupid problem since stupid can be quite deadly, but due to all the protection people have in this country, I'm sure that in the end we will be the last ones standing, I mean us Americans, thank God.

CHAPTER 8
An Expert Way

I have studied martial arts for most of my life.

Lesson number one—never put into motion any part of your body before looking first.

Lesson number two—always know what and who is around you at all times.

It's called having a total level of awareness.

Well, hell, everywhere I look I see people doing just the opposite. Have you ever noticed that in the scary movies, the victim almost always has to walk backward without looking? That way he or she can accidentally walk right up to the big bad monster; otherwise they would turn around and see him and run, or better yet, just shoot him. But then the movie would be over, and that wouldn't be any fun.

Just like the ladies in the store in the last chapter, and most of the people I have talked about in this book, they don't have a high level of awareness or, for that matter, any awareness at all. They're basically unconscious and unaware of what's going on around them; thus they appear stupid, because that's what they are. Unconscious, unaware, and stupid.

It doesn't take a mental giant or martial arts training to know that if you are unaware of where you are going, then you will probably end up somewhere that you don't know.

Or better yet, if you are unaware of what's going on around you, then you may end up appearing stupid, like the ladies in the store, totally unaware, and that's no way to go through life. It is just stupid.

But that's exactly what you see in this nation today— a lot of people oblivious to the way they are going to where they are going but seemingly knowing where, but not why, like herd mentality in humans.

Like being in a hurry but not knowing why, just

conditioned, without reason, like a trail of ants.

Now, I would just bet that if you were to do a survey of the average Iraqi civilian, you would find that they are more conscious than we are due to the fact that we have been safe for so long and we have forgotten what it's like to have to have your wits about you. Unlike over in Iraq where if you don't have your wits due to being unconscious you could be killed.

There are numerous theorists, scholars, and writers who are theorizing that the human enterprise is going to be given a higher level of consciousness in the year 2012 and for different reasons. One is due to the fact that we are well into the information age, and the World Wide Web is generating a global consciousness, which I think is wonderful, but as for me, I will focus on being conscious and aware right now of all that is or all that I can.

It's a practiced thing, to be aware, I mean. If you practice, every time you go anywhere, observing everything you can and taking notice so that later you can recall, and do this on a daily basis, you will find that, in time, you will become better and better at it, thus aware.

If you live in the city, and you haven't been around animals very much, then you have probably never noticed how when animals group together in larger than normal flocks, herds, or schools, they become less aware of their surroundings. It's as if they rely on each other to see danger coming, or perhaps there's just safety in numbers so that when the big predator comes, he gets the other guy. At any rate that's exactly what you see people doing in the world today.

The more people you have in an area, the dumber they are, just like animals; it's called herd behavior in humans.

But not me, as I don't like being around large numbers of people, so perhaps I'm more like a wolf, and the rest are the sheep. Well, that makes sense, since I would rather be a wolf than a sheep. That way I would get to do all the chasing, and they would have to do the running.

But no matter what I am, I will always try to be the best that I can.

Driving is the same as walking or pushing a shopping

cart in that you maneuver through with awareness, respect, and humility, at all times, period, or you could get shot, and mark my words, it's just a matter of time before that's exactly what's going to happen where I live, since these idiots aren't going to stop being idiots until it does.

But such is life in the animal kingdom. When the numbers get to be too great, Mother Nature will kick in and issue a disease, or a natural catastrophe to reduce them, as to protect herself. Humans are supposed to not need her to do that since we have a brain, but that's exactly what you see in the world today, huge die-offs of people and mass extinctions of animals are just beginning, with many already gone.

The human enterprise is heading for disaster, with more and more people in the world today, and they are dumber and dumber, as the stage is being set.

If you look at this perspective as a zoologist, then you see that there have been many mass extinctions on this planet over time, and this time is no different in the eyes of Mother Nature. She has a way of keeping things in balance, and when a species overpopulates and overcomes the small stuff like disease, famine, volcanoes, tsunamis, and hurricanes, she will keep on trying until she gets the job done, like global warming, a global problem, and I think that terrorism, too, is just another piece of the puzzle coming together.

Yes, animals can overcome disease; they spread away from the population, thereby isolating themselves and starting over, while the rest die of the disease.

But that's gloomy, and no one wants to hear that, so I will just stick with the stupid people in Montana since we have our share of them, and they pretty much represent the rest of the nation, as that's where most of them come from.

Plus they're more interesting anyway, like the lady who came to the Campground Store and wanted to buy a can of Raid bug spray, since she heard that it's smart to spray down while camping in Montana so you won't get bit by mosquitoes. She's priceless.

Special thanks to Mom and Dad for instilling in me the desire to ponder that which is known, and to seek out the mysteries of the universe. May someday we have answers to them all.

And thanks to you, for reading.

Breinigsville, PA USA
03 November 2010

248577BV00002B/294/P